Moonflute

by Audrey Wood

Illustrated by Don Wood

HARCOURT BRACE JOVANOVICH, PUBLISHERS

San Diego   New York   London

Moonflute was originally published by Green Tiger Press.

Library of Congress Cataloging-in-Publication Data
Wood, Audrey
Moonflute.
Summary: A moonbeam turns into a magic flute
and takes Firen on a journey through the night sky
to find out what the moon has done with her lost sleep.
[1. Flute—Fiction.   2. Moon—Fiction]   I. Wood,
Don, 1945–   ill. II. Title.
PZ7.W846Mo   1986   [E]   86-4666
ISBN 0-15-255337-1

HBJ

Printed in the United States of America
B C D E

For Edwina Cook Brewer,
the oldest and the wisest

On a night when the moon was full of itself, full of restless dreams and wide-awake thoughts, a girl by the name of Firen could not sleep. She could not sleep because the night was hot and shining with full-moon magic. She could not sleep because the moon was pretending to be the sun, dressing up the world of night in a silvery day.

"Firen . . . Firen . . . Firen . . ." the bullfrogs, crickets, and katydids seemed to call, "come out, come out, come out and look around."

The girl tossed this way and that on her rumpled bed. She looked up at the moon through her wide-open window and said: "What have you done with my sleep, moon? Did you hide it under the jasmine bush? Did you send it to the creek to catch a fish?"

But the moon did not answer. It sat in the sky, sparkling and milky white.

Firen shook her finger at the moon and said: "I want my sleep back, moon. I will go out in the night and find it."

Softly, on tiptoe bare feet, the girl slipped out of her window and into the night.

Honeysuckle vines smelling as sweet as syrup filled the air. A cool breeze found its way through the hot summer night, lifting Firen's hair and tickling her ears. Great-grandfather trees twisted their branches against the moonlit sky. Garlands of moss hung from their limbs, looking like old men's beards swaying in the breeze. The moon lit up the dew-sprinkled grass like diamond dust—everything was strange and eerie and different at night.

"Who? Who? Who?" an owl hooted from the nearby forest. "Who? Who?"

Firen waited and listened. She could feel her heart beating like a bird caught in her chest, flapping its wings, trying to get out.

Then she raised her arms to the sky and cupped her hands so that the moon seemed to rest between her palms.

"Where is my sleep?" Firen whispered. "Give it back to me."

Then the moon began its sorcery. First it quivered like a ball of white jelly, then it glowed with a startling brightness, growing larger and larger. Just when Firen thought it would certainly explode, a sliver of light jumped out of the moon's center and streaked toward earth.

The moon has sprung a leak, Firen thought. *It is losing its whiteness.*

The girl watched the moonbeam falling through the sky toward her. Before she could blink, the light landed, flat and true and quivering in her outstretched hands. Firen slowly brought the moon-treasure down to her eyes so that she might have a better look. It glowed like an ember, casting a brilliant light upon her face.

Could this be my sleep? She wondered, *Did the moon spit it back at me?*

The girl touched her fingers to the shining moon-ray. It was cool, and about as thick as a good throwing stick. Unlike any light she had ever seen before, the moon-ray was solid. When Firen turned the light-stick over, she discovered a row of seven evenly spaced holes. Without thinking, she brought the light up to her lips, placed her fingers on the holes, and blew.

The moonflute made music—a special kind of music. It was not the "tweedle-dee-dee toot" that just any old wood-wind pipe makes. This music trickled like water over rocks, clinked like crystal chimes in the wind, and jingled like brass bells on a sleigh. There were also sounds she had never heard before—the music of billowing clouds, the songs of migrating birds, and the sighs of blooming flowers.

And even better and more wonderful, good smells followed the moonflute's music—sweet cinnamon cakes, crisp leaves burning in bonfires, apples baking, and crushed pine needles. The music filled Firen's heart with happiness; it made her long to see the things she could only hear and smell.

As the girl played the flute, she looked up at the face of the moon, and her fingers began to tingle. The tingling spread through her arms and rushed down to her toes, making her lighter than a feather. Slowly, she rose into the air, then faster and faster until she was standing in the sky.

Firen looked at the world below her. Trees were now dark shapes casting stringy shadows across the earth. Her own home, where her mother and father lay sleeping, became a dollhouse, the fields and pastures, her own patchwork quilt.

"Good-bye, Father and Mother," she called from the sky. "The moon is showing me a way to find my sleep."

Firen flew like a bird without wings. In a very short time, she could see the nearby town. Buildings large and small popped up out of dimly lit streets.

The town was crowded with shadows—rectangular shadows sneaking out from under stores and houses; triangular shadows falling on rooftops; square, oblong, and zig-zagity shadows making patterns wherever they pleased.

As Firen soared over the church, a flock of pigeons burst out of the steeple, crying in alarm and showering the sky with ruffled feathers. Firen raced above the streets, swooshing past fire hydrants, street lamps, and park benches.

"Yeeowwll meeeyowell. . . ."

Firen heard cats whining and hissing in the streets below, their shrieks filling the sleeping town with shivers and goose bumps. Flying over a picket fence and down an alley, she followed the cat noises. Firen stopped above a black shadow where the cats were hiding and crossed her legs in the air.

Did the moon toss my sleep to the cats? she wondered. *Are the cats fighting over it, chasing it like a mouse?*

Firen leaned down closer. She could see the cats now, but they were not fighting or chasing her sleep. They were sitting on their furry haunches, chewing catnip and looking at the full moon through diamond cat eyes.

Firen raised the pipe to her lips and flew through the sky, leaving the town far behind. She listened to the moonflute's music. It was sounding like waves and smelling of salt spray.

Now when Firen glanced below, she did not see mountains, valleys, fields, or plains; she saw an ocean that went on and on with no beginning or end. Firen blinked her eyes in amazement—so much water!

The bright and silent moon, high above the water, made a path of shining light over the choppy sea. Firen dove down to the moonlit path and flew above it, snatching handfuls of sea foam from the tops of rolling waves. Suddenly the waves parted. Great whales raised their barnacled backs from the water, spraying fountains of pearly foam from their blowholes. Firen shot up higher into the air, laughing and wet, sprinkled with sea spray.

Did the moon toss my sleep to the whales? Firen wondered. *Are they teaching my sleep how to swim and dive to the bottom of the ocean?*

Swooping low over the whales' gigantic heads, she watched them splashing and diving, playing hide-and-seek with the moonlight.

The whales do not have my sleep, Firen thought.

The whales stopped frolicking and listened while
Firen played her moonflute, and when she finished her
song, they sang their own song back. Musical gurglings,
high-pitched whistles, squeaks and trillings filled the sea-salt air.

When the whales finished, Firen curtsied in the sky, bowing her
head in admiration.

With a splash of foam, the great creatures dove for the bottom of the dark sea,
leaving Firen alone.

"Where will I find my sleep?" she asked. "It was not in my room, it was not in
the town, it was not in the hills and valleys I left so far behind, and it is not here
in the deep ocean. Where can it be?"

Once again Firen brought the moonflute to her lips and played as she flew into
the sky. This time the music spoke of land and smelled of honey-flowers and ripe
mangoes hanging from trees, ready to be eaten. Firen looked below into a dark,
tangled jungle.

Drifting down to the nearest tree she hovered above its branches.

Why has the moonflute brought me here? she wondered.

Fireflies flicked their lantern tails on and off, great bats darted through leathery leaves, tree frogs by the millions croaked and creeked.

"Ee eeee eeeee . . ." a noise sounded below the jungle's canopy. "Eee eeeee ee."

Circling above the trees, Firen soon found a small opening into the dense jungle. She spiraled down, stopping above the misty ground, and looked around at the world beneath the treetops.

Ghostly white and gnarled tree trunks crowded close together. Fat vines hung from their limbs, looping like giant snakes from tree to tree. Not a breath of wind stirred the air.

"Eeee eee . . ." the sound called out again, but this time it was very near. Firen squinted her eyes, trying to see, but the jungle kept its secret. Rising up, the girl flew into the tangled vines and branches—now she could see hundreds of monkeys,

a city of monkeys!

   Did the moon toss my sleep to the monkeys? She wondered, *Are they swinging through the branches with it, throwing it back and forth like a ball?*

But when Firen flew among the trees, she found the monkeys did not have her sleep. They were chattering and pointing at the full moon that peeped brightly through the dark leaves above. In the fork of a large tree, a family of monkeys sat on a platform made of twigs and moss, scratching each others' backs and fanning themselves with banana leaves. When they saw Firen standing in the air, they pursed their lips and shook their heads.

"Eeee ee," the baby monkey cried, clinging to its mother's back. The mother wrapped her arms around her baby, rocking gently back and forth, back and forth. Feeling warm and cozy, the little monkey snuggled close to her breast. The father monkey swung down on a vine and sat beside the mother, putting his arm around her waist. The two monkeys watched their baby blink its eyes, yawn, then slowly fall asleep.

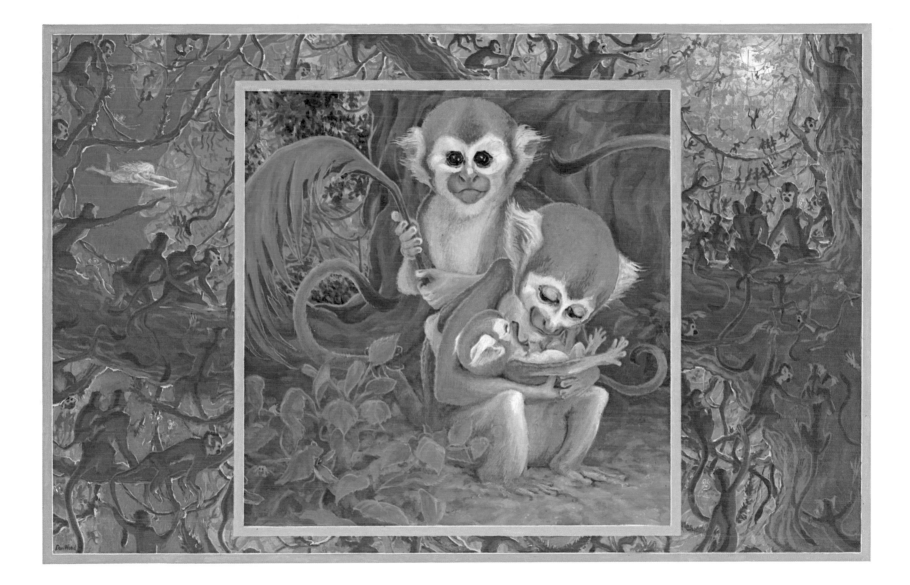

Firen thought about her father and mother. She remembered the story Father had read that night, the kisses Mother had given her, and the song they had all sung together. She thought about her home, and her room with her bed of rumpled covers—they all seemed so far away, so long ago.

As Firen remembered these good things, her fingers started to play the moon-flute. She could hear the crickets, bullfrogs, and katydids. She could smell the honeysuckle vines and moss-covered trees near her home.

All the monkeys watched as Firen rose above their leafy city and disappeared into the night. They listened until the music faded away.

Soon Firen was not flying—she was speeding through the sky like a rocket firecracker, whizzing over mountain ranges, bursting through clouds, sizzling over canyons, valleys, cities large and small. In the time it takes to snuff a candle, Firen came speeding through the night to her very own town. A street cleaner looked up from his broom and thought he saw a star falling from the sky. He ran to the bell tower and rang the bells, waking the sleepy town and calling out, "Look! Look! Wake up! A star is falling from the sky!"

But Firen was already out of sight and slowing down, going down, down to the dew-sprinkled grass, down through her open window and onto her very own bed.

She listened to the village bells ringing in the night and smiled. Firen's father and mother, awakened by the bells, tiptoed into her room. They yawned, kissed her on the forehead, and straightened her covers.

Firen remembered the moonflute. She wanted to play it for her parents and surprise them, but when she brought it to her lips—it was gone! It was not in her hand, covers, or clothes. Firen wondered, *Did I drop the moonflute in the dew-sprinkled grass?*

The girl rubbed her sleepy eyes and looked at the moon shining through the window.

"Good night, moon," she said. "You took away my sleep, but you gave me a magic way to get it back."

Firen snuggled down under the quilt, closed her eyes slowly, and thought, *Tomorrow I will look for the moonflute, and tomorrow I will find it.*

And then she fell asleep.

The paintings in this book were done in oil on pressed board.
The text type was set on the Linotron 202 in Goudy Old Style by Thompson Type, San Diego, California.
The display type was hand-lettered by Lester G. Bast, Jr.
Color separations were made by Heinz Weber, Inc., Los Angeles, California
Printed by Holyoke Lithograph Company, Springfield, Massachusetts.
Bound by A. Horowitz & Son, Bookbinders, Fairfield, New Jersey.
Production supervision by Warren Wallerstein.
Designed by Francesca M. Smith.